This igloo book
belongs to:

....

igloobooks

Published in 2023
First published in the UK by Igloo Books Ltd
An imprint of Igloo Books Ltd
Cottage Farm, NN6 0BJ, UK
Owned by Bonnier Books
Sveavägen 56, Stockholm, Sweden
www.igloobooks.com

0223 001
2 4 6 8 10 9 7 5 3 1
ISBN 978-1-80108-469-7

Written by Stephanie Moss
Illustrated by Sejung Kim

Designed by Alex Alexandrou
Edited by Hannah Campling

Printed and manufactured in China

Cuddle Me

igloobooks

CLICK-CLICK went the lights.
There was darkness everywhere.
Spooky shadows creeped.
Bunny said, "I'm really scared!"

"Cuddle Fluffy Teddy," said Mum.
"Squeeze him very tight."

"See, the dark's not scary!"
Then, she gave a kiss goodnight.

TOYS

Bedtime wasn't scary with her teddy by her side.

One day, something happened. "It's a new toy!" Bunny cried.

In the gloomy toybox, Fluffy Teddy felt alone.

"It's dark in here," he whispered.
"How will I sleep on my own?"

The other toys were snoring.
They weren't frightened at all.
So, Fluffy Teddy tiptoed through
the room and down the hall.

He ran to Bunny's brother's room and peeked around the door. But he didn't need a goodnight cuddle any more.

Bunny's little sister
didn't make a single noise.
He whispered, "No one needs me here.
They've all got their own toys!"

He looked into the darkness and thought of his new bed. "There must be somewhere safe and warm that I can sleep instead."

PLOD PLOD

down the stairs he went.
"Is anybody here?"

He snuggled by the coats,
but then he covered up his ears.

"What's that creaking? Ahh, a groan! A ghost is in the house!"

When Fluffy Teddy looked, he saw that it was just a mouse.

"The cupboard in the kitchen's warm."
But as he closed his eyes,
Fluffy Teddy saw a monster
swoop down from the sky!

It landed by the window and let out a creepy howl.

He ran away and didn't see the friendly hooting owl.

Fluffy Teddy climbed the stairs while looking all around.
He almost got to Bunny's room, but heard another sound.

SPLUTTER, SNIFFLE, SNUFFLE!
He said, "Ahh! What could that be?
Another scary monster? No...

... a teddy, just like me!"

Her name
was Tiny Teddy.
She was looking
very sad.

She felt scared in the
darkness, just like
Fluffy Teddy had.

"I live in Bunny's
sister's room.
We cuddle close
all night.
A bad dream woke
her up, and only
Mum could make
things right."

"Don't worry," Fluffy Teddy said,
"I know just what to do,
because I've got a secret...

I'm still scared
of the dark too!"

They tiptoed through the darkness,
squeezing on each other's paws,
until they reached her bedroom,
and they slipped inside the door.

They climbed onto the pillow, and they settled down in bed.

Then, Bunny's sister came back, and Mum kissed her on the head.

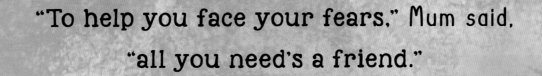

"To help you face your fears," Mum said,
"all you need's a friend."

They smiled and cuddled closer.
Then, they fell asleep... The end!